W9-ALV-493

for Lydie and Ingo

First edition 2020

Library of Congress Catalog Card Number pending
ISBN 978-0-7636-9060-1

19 20 21 22 23 24 CCP 10 9 8 7 6 5 4 3 2 1

Printed in Shenzhen, Guangdong, China

This book was hand-lettered by the author-illustrator.
The illustrations were done in watercolor.

Candlewick Press
99 Dover Street
Somerville, Massachusetts 02144

visit us at www.candlewick.com

MAMA
BABY

Chris Raschka

CANDLEWICK PRESS

MAMA

BABY

MAMA

BABY

CLAP CLAP

CLAP CLAP

BYE-BYE

BYE-BYE

PEEK-A-BOO

PEEK-A-BOO

PAT-A-CAKE

PAT-A-CAKE

MAMA?

UP UP

BYE-BYE